Disney PRESENTS A PIXAR FILM

THE INCREDIBLES
CALLING ALL SUPERS!

Random House 🏠 New York

This reusable sticker book is your ticket to an incredible adventure. Join Bob Parr and his family as they protect their city by fighting the evil Syndrome. Use your stickers to complete the activities.

You can use the page entitled "My Story" at the end of this book to create your own adventures with your reusable stickers.

Have an adult help you remove the perforated sticker pages.

Random House 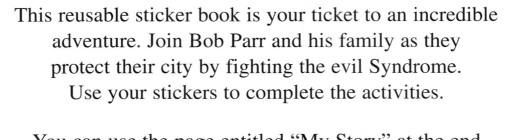 New York

Copyright © 2004 Disney Enterprises, Inc./Pixar Animation Studios. All rights reserved under International and Pan-American Copyright Conventions. Published in the United States by Random House Children's Books, a division of Random House, Inc., New York, NY 10019 and simultaneously in Canada by Random House of Canada Limited, Toronto, in conjunction with Disney Enterprises, Inc. RANDOM HOUSE and colophon are registered trademarks of Random House, Inc.

ISBN: 0-7364-2287-0
www.randomhouse.com/kids/disney

MANUFACTURED IN ITALY   10 9 8 7 6 5 4 3

Produced by Phidal Publishing Inc.
5740 Ferrier, Montreal, Canada H4P 1M7

SUPER RELOCATION PROGRAM

Use your stickers to reveal each character's secret identity.

DASH

JACK-JACK

FROZONE

ELASTIGIRL

MR. INCREDIBLE

VIOLET

HEROES AND VILLAINS

Use your stickers to answer the questions.

SAVING METROVILLE

Use your stickers to decorate the scene.

MIGHTY MATCH-UP
Use your stickers to make the right match.

SECRET IDENTITY

Match each character to the color that reveals his or her true identity.

THE GOOD AND THE BAD

Use your stickers to identify each character.

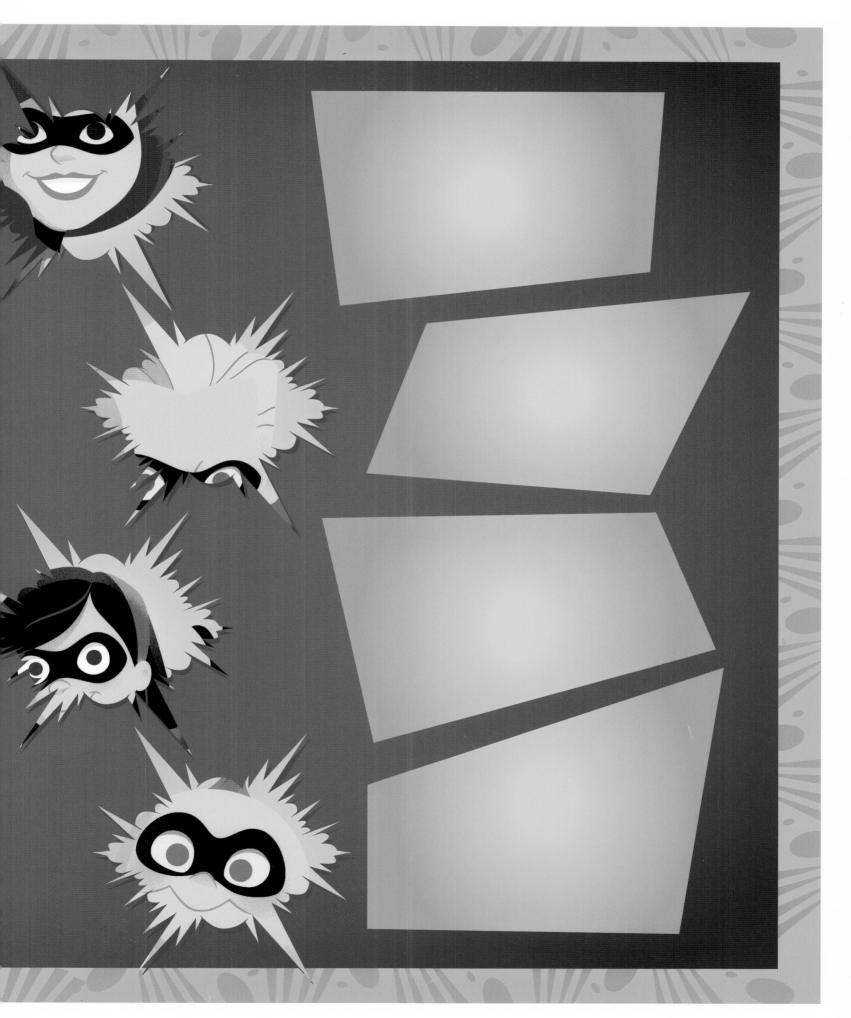

STOP SYNDROME!

Look closely at this scene.

Now use your stickers to make the scene below look like the one above.